WORSE THAN THEY THOUGHT

"Okay," Mr. Parker said. "Who wants to pump the life back into this old ball?"

Zach volunteered, and started pumping away. The kids got excited, thinking there was still a chance they could have a game today. But something wasn't right. The air was coming out of the ball just as quickly as Zach was getting it in.

Finally, he gave up.

"Uh-oh," he said.

Then he brought the ball up to his ear and listened. "There's a hole in this ball, right near the laces," Zach said. "I can hear the air coming out of it. Sorry, everybody." He shrugged. "Looks like no game today."

It was as if the air went out of all of them at once.

Mateo said he had a ball the same size at home and would be happy to bring it to school tomorrow. That made everyone feel a little better. It just didn't explain how the hole ended up in the football.

THE ZACH & ZOE MYSTERIES

THE FOOTBALL FIASCO

Mike Lupica

illustrated by

Chris Danger

Puffin Books

PUFFIN BOOKS
An imprint of Penguin Random House LLC
375 Hudson Street
New York, NY 10014

Published simultaneously in the United States of America by Puffin Books and
Philomel Books, imprints of Penguin Random House LLC, 2018

Text copyright © 2018 by Mike Lupica
Illustrations copyright © 2018 by Chris Danger

LIBRARY OF CONGRESS CATALOGING-IN-PUBLICATION DATA
Names: Lupica, Mike, author. | Danger, Chris, illustrator.
Title: The football fiasco / Mike Lupica ; illustrated by Chris Danger.
Description: New York, New York : Puffin Books, 2018. | Series: Zach and Zoe
mysteries ; [3] | Summary: "Zach and Zoe find their recess football
deflated from a hole near the laces, and set off in search of clues to
discover how it happened"— Provided by publisher.
Identifiers: LCCN 2018013788| ISBN 9780425289433 (paperback)
ISBN 9780425289426 (hardcover)
Subjects: | CYAC: Mystery and detective stories. | Football—Fiction.
Schools—Fiction. | Brothers and sisters—Fiction. | Twins—Fiction.
BISAC: JUVENILE FICTION / Sports & Recreation / Football.
JUVENILE FICTION / Mysteries & Detective Stories.
JUVENILE FICTION / School & Education.
Classification: LCC PZ7.L97914 Foo 2018
DDC [Fic]—dc23
LC record available at https://lccn.loc.gov/2018013788

Puffin Books ISBN 9780425289433

Printed in the United States of America

1 3 5 7 9 10 8 6 4 2

Design by Maria Fazio
Text set in Fournier MT Std

For the Lupica boys, Chris and Alex and
Zach, and all the other participants in our
family's annual Turkey Bowl.

ONE

Zach and Zoe Walker were getting ready for one of their favorite parts of the school day at Middletown Elementary:

The touch football game they played with some of their classmates at recess.

Not everybody chose to play football at recess. Some of the other kids played basketball. Some kicked a soccer ball around. Some played on the jungle gym, or played freeze tag.

But Zach and Zoe were even more excited to play football than usual today, because it was the Friday before Thanksgiving. That meant it was almost time for the big Walker family football game they called the Turkey Bowl, before they sat down for Thanksgiving dinner.

Now it was just a few days before Thanksgiving break, and Zach and Zoe couldn't wait to get outside and practice for the big game.

"Remember how last year's Turkey Bowl ended?" Zach said to his twin sister.

"How could I forget?" she said. "You're the one who keeps reminding me how Grandpa Richie threw you the game-winning pass!"

"The only person happier than me last year was Grandpa Richie," Zach said.

"He's the one who came up with the idea of the game in the first place," said

Zoe. "It's why he always has more fun than anybody in our family."

That day, Zach was starting as quarterback for one of the teams. He had the best arm in their grade. But their friends Malik and Mateo got to play quarterback, too. So did Kari and Zoe. The teams were different every day. The only thing that never changed was their sad-looking old ball. It had been around since before Zach and Zoe started elementary school.

The ball really wasn't much to look at. But they were used to it by now, almost as if it were an old friend. It had "NFL" written on the side, for National Football League. It also said "Junior Touchdown." The laces were worn down, and the seams were loose, but it was still their ball.

Every time they played with it, Lily would make fun of the ball, telling them it should have "Senior" written on it instead of "Junior," because it looked older than all of them put together. She was always complaining that it was time for the school to get them a new one. But it was all they had. To Zach and Zoe, the condition of the ball didn't matter, as long as they could use it to play.

There were eight players in all, four to a side. It was Zach and Zoe's turn to pick teams. Zach chose Malik first, and then Kari Stuart and Brian Koppelman. Zoe took Mateo and Lily and finally another boy in their class, Jimmy Evans. Jimmy was a small, thin boy who wore glasses. He didn't say much, but he always joined them for recess football.

The most important rule they had came from Zach and Zoe's dad. It was something he always told them about sports.

"Have fun! If you don't enjoy yourselves, then sports are about as much fun as cleaning your room."

They played nonstop for the next twenty minutes of recess. Zoe's team ended up with the ball in the last drive of a tie game. By then, she was playing quarterback. On the second-to-last play, she'd thrown the ball to Jimmy, just because she couldn't remember anybody throwing it to him the whole game. Jimmy was open, but he took his eyes off the ball at the last second and dropped it.

All of a sudden, the bell sounded for the end of recess. They had time for one last play. Mateo broke away from Zach, and Zoe threw him a touchdown pass that won the game for their team.

Even though Zach was on the other team, he was the first to run up to his sister for their special high five. The one that began with them bumping elbows and hips and then finally jumping into the air. It was the same today as in any game they played, whether they were teammates or not. As much as they both loved to compete, they loved each other more. No matter who won or lost, nothing ever beat that.

As they walked back inside, Zoe thought that Jimmy looked a little sad, even though their team had won.

She walked up alongside him. "Why do you look so sad?" Zoe asked. "We won!"

"Nobody ever throws me the ball," he said. "And when you finally did today, I dropped it."

"I dropped one a few plays before that," Zoe said. "It happens to everybody. Zach's really good at football, and even he dropped a couple today. It's all part of the game."

She smiled at him, suddenly wanting to cheer him up.

"The best thing about recess is that there's always another game next time," she said.

"Maybe you're right," Jimmy said, but he didn't sound convinced. Then he walked ahead of her into the school building.

Zach had been walking behind with Mateo, but he caught up with Zoe as she was walking through the door.

"You looked pretty good throwing that ball around today," Zach said.

"Maybe I should be one of the starting quarterbacks in the Turkey Bowl," she said.

"I thought you liked being a wide receiver better."

"Maybe I was just trying to fake you out the way I did a couple of times in the game today," Zoe said, winking.

"Or *maybe* you were just trying to be mysterious," Zach said, "as usual."

Anybody who knew Zoe Walker knew how much she loved a good mystery. Any kind of mystery.

But neither she nor her brother knew that the latest mystery was about to start.

TWO

The weekend flew by, and now it was Monday. Zach and Zoe were having lunch in the school cafeteria. While they were eating, they overheard one of the lunch aides complaining to Ms. Moriarty. With a frown, she grumbled about how dirty some of the kids were when they came back inside after recess.

The lunch aide's name was Ms. Gundy, and this wasn't the first time they'd heard her complaining about something. It was why Zach and Zoe thought of her as Ms. Grumpy, though they never shared the nickname with anybody else.

"They should just stay inside and study," they heard Ms. Gundy say to Ms. Moriarty now.

"I actually think the children can sometimes learn as much from sports as they can from books," Ms. Moriarty said. "And besides, being outside before the weather gets too cold always does them good."

"What could they possibly learn from sports?" Ms. Gundy said, sneering.

"A lot of things," Ms. Moriarty said. "They learn about hard work, being on a team, and getting back up after you get knocked down."

"Well, from the looks of them when they get back inside," Ms. Gundy said, "all they do on that field is get knocked down."

Ms. Moriarty looked past Ms. Gundy

and saw Zach and Zoe looking back at her. She winked at them.

"So if they do get knocked down as much as you say," Ms. Moriarty replied, "just think how much they've learned!"

"One of these days," Ms. Gundy said, sounding grumpier than ever, "somebody should hide that football of theirs so they're forced to stay inside and study."

There were always two footballs available in the storage room for recess. The fifth graders had already finished their lunch, and took the football they usually played with before heading outside. The fourth graders normally played with the fifth graders, but they had a class trip scheduled for that afternoon at the town firehouse, and were leaving right after lunch. And the kindergartners and first and second graders didn't play football.

Zach finished his lunch and headed to the storage room next to the cafeteria to get their football for recess. The athletic equipment was kept in a wire bin. Piled inside were soccer balls, basketballs, a volleyball, Nerf balls, and Wiffle balls. Then Zach noticed something. At the top sat their NFL Junior Touchdown football. Except now the ball was completely deflated. Flat as a pancake, as his mom liked to say.

In that moment, Zach felt almost as deflated as the ball.

There were lots of other balls in the bin. But no other footballs. It meant there wouldn't be a game at recess today unless Mr. Parker or somebody at school could pump up the ball or quickly find another one.

When Zach came outside with the deflated ball, Malik looked confused. "Are you sure that's ours?" he asked.

Zach sadly showed him the NFL logo.

"I'm surprised it lasted as long as it did," Lily said, rolling her eyes.

"Could somebody else have used the football after school on Friday?" Mateo asked. "Maybe they did something that took the air out of it."

"It's possible," Zoe said. "But even if it was an accident, whoever it was should have told us about it. Especially if they know how much we like to use that ball!"

"I'll go find Mr. Parker or Ms. Moriarty and see if they can pump it up," said Zach.

He ran over to where Ms. Moriarty was standing on the basketball court and showed her the deflated ball. "Let me go look for Mr. Parker," she said. "He'll know what to do." Mr. Parker was the school's cus-todian. Ms. Moriarity went looking for him, and a few minutes later, she returned to the basketball court. This time, Mr. Parker walked alongside her. He was holding a small pump with a needle attached to it.

"This ought to save the day," he said.

"Mr. Parker to the rescue!" Zoe cheered.

"Okay," Mr. Parker said. "Who wants to pump the life back into this old ball?"

Zach volunteered, and started pumping away. The kids got excited, thinking there was still a chance they could have a game today. But something wasn't right. The air was coming out of the ball just as quickly as Zach was getting it in.

Finally, he gave up.

"Uh-oh," he said.

Then he brought the ball up to his ear and listened. "There's a hole in this ball, right near the laces," Zach said. "I can hear the air coming out of it. Sorry, everybody." He shrugged. "Looks like no game today."

It was as if the air went out of all of them at once.

Ms. Moriarty looked at her watch and told them recess was nearly over. She suggested maybe someone could bring a ball to school the next day and they could have a few more games before Thanksgiving break.

Mateo said he had a ball the same size at home and would be happy to bring it to school tomorrow. That made everyone feel a little better. It just didn't explain how the hole ended up in the football.

Zoe waited until they were on the bus home to talk about the mystery of their football with Zach. She and her brother did their best thinking when it was just the two of them. Sometimes it was as if they were using the same brain.

"Do you think it might have been Ms. Grumpy?" Zoe said, keeping her voice low.

"I know she said she wanted us to stay inside and study during recess," Zach said. "But I can't believe she'd actually put a hole in our football."

"But the storage room *is* right next to the cafeteria," Zoe pointed out. "And the ball was still fine when you put it back in there after Friday's game."

Zach saw his sister frown the way she did when she was focusing really hard on a problem. It was the same expression she had doing a math equation, or while thinking about a brand-new mystery.

"You don't really think she'd poke a hole in the ball," Zach said. "Do you?"

Zoe sighed. "I guess I don't," she said. "Ms. Moriarty says that as grumpy as she sounds sometimes, Ms. Gundy's actually a really good person. But you know what Mom says when we're trying to solve a mystery. You have to look at all the possibilities."

"What about Lily?" Zach offered. "She's always making fun of how old our ball is. Maybe this was her way of getting the school to buy us a new one."

"I guess we have to put her on our list of suspects," Zoe said, "even if she's one of our friends."

When they got off the bus, their mom, Tess, was waiting for them. She had a huge smile on her face, as usual. Zach and Zoe always noticed. Every single day they got off the bus, their mom looked so happy to see them. It was as if she hadn't seen them for weeks, even though they'd only been gone since breakfast.

She also knew them as well as they knew themselves.

"I see two very serious faces," she said, suddenly concerned. "What's up?"

"Not up," Zoe said. "Something happened at school that kind of dragged us *down*."

They told her about the football as they walked into the house.

"Well, it's a good thing I made your favorite cookies, then," said Tess. It was the only thing that could make them feel better at a time like this.

They sat down at the kitchen table for oatmeal raisin cookies and milk. Then their mom said, "You think somebody intentionally punched a hole in the ball?"

"Nothing else makes sense, Mom," Zoe said.

"It's not like that time your car went over a nail and put a hole in the tire," Zach said. "Footballs don't run over nails."

"So who do you think could have done it?" Zoe asked their mom.

Tess smiled again. "Hey," she said, throwing up her hands, "you two are the detectives in the family."

"Somebody must have had a very good reason," Zach said.

"A good reason to keep us from playing football at recess?" said Zoe, doubtful.

"We have to find the person," Zach said, "and then we have to find the reason."

For the first time since they'd gotten on the bus, it was Zoe who was smiling.

"Two mysteries in one!" she said, her eyes wide with excitement.

Zach glanced over at his mom.

"Uh-oh," he said. "Here we go again."

THREE

The Walker twins finally got to play some football later that afternoon. It was in the backyard, with their dad and Grandpa Richie before dinner. But only for practice. It was already Monday and there were just three days left before the big game.

At one point, Grandpa Richie threw a long pass to Zach. He caught it like it was another game-winner in the Turkey Bowl.

"Boy gets his blazing speed from me,"

Grandpa Richie said to his son, the twins' dad, Danny Walker. He was home early from the television station where he worked.

"And what did I get from you, Grandpa?" Zoe asked.

"You got your own blazing speed," Grandpa Richie replied.

"And what did they get from *me*?" Zach and Zoe's dad asked.

Grandpa Richie scratched his head, as if trying to come up with something. "Can I get back to you on that one?" They all laughed.

At the dinner table, Zach and Zoe filled their dad and Grandpa Richie in on what happened to their football.

"You'll figure it out," their dad said finally.

Zoe met his eyes. "How can you be so sure?"

"Because once the two of you are on a case, you *always* figure things out eventually," he said.

"You're right about that," Zoe said. "We never give up."

"Never!" Zach echoed.

"Wait, I've got it!" Grandpa Richie said, snapping his finger. "I finally figured out something they got from you, Danny— their determination!"

"And what did they get from me?" asked Tess.

Grandpa Richie didn't hesitate.

"Their great minds," he said.

They all laughed again. It didn't take a great mind to know how much fun it was being a part of this family.

FOUR

Mateo brought his own junior-sized football to school on Tuesday, as promised. But it didn't matter, because it rained all morning. Outdoor recess was canceled, and so was their game.

But Zach and Zoe weren't giving up on solving "the football fiasco," as they called it. They had a problem on their hands, and they loved solving problems. They got to challenge their brains the way they challenged themselves in sports.

"Mysteries are like taking tests," Zoe said to Zach.

"Just more difficult sometimes," said Zach.

"Hey," said Zoe, "where would the challenge be if it were easy?"

Before they walked into the cafeteria for lunch, Zach and Zoe asked Ms. Moriarty if they could take another look in the storage room.

"Wait, don't tell me," she said, grinning. "You two are looking for something you might have missed."

"How did you know?" Zoe asked.

"Just had a hunch," Ms. Moriarty said, winking at Zoe. Then she wished them luck finding any clues.

Once inside the storage room, Zach and Zoe headed over to the wire bin filled with balls. At the top sat their deflated Junior Touchdown football. Zach picked it up and shook his head sadly. Mr. Parker said there might be a way to patch up the ball and save it without the school having to order a new one, which could take a week or more to arrive. But that wasn't doing them any good right now.

Zach and Zoe tipped over the bin and the other balls came tumbling out, along with something else. . . .

A pair of eyeglasses.

Zoe picked up the glasses and showed them to Zach. "A clue!"

"Can you tell if they might belong to a grown-up or somebody our age?" Zach asked.

"I hate to say it," Zoe said, "but they look a lot like Lily's."

"And remember, she's still on our list of suspects," said Zach. "Lily isn't shy about how she feels about our old ball."

"Do you think she could have put a hole in our football? Maybe her glasses were hanging in her shirt, and they fell out when she bent over to put the ball back in the bin," Zoe said.

"Remember the time she broke her glasses playing in our football game?" Zach said. "She said her mom always made her bring a backup pair and keep them in her cubby."

They still didn't want to believe that Lily would put a hole in their football. But to prove she hadn't, they knew they were going to have to find out if she was missing a pair of eyeglasses.

"It's like we added another mystery to our mystery!" Zoe said. "This one is about a missing pair of glasses."

Zach laughed. "How many mysteries do we have to solve this week?"

They had to admit the glasses might not be a clue at all. Or they might be the best clue they had. After lunch, they returned to their classroom and noticed Lily was wearing her glasses. And they *did* look a lot like the ones they'd found.

Zoe turned the glasses in to Ms. Moriarty, who asked the class if anybody was missing a pair. Zach and Zoe looked around. They paid close attention to Lily, in case she raised her hand. They also noticed Jimmy in the back row, wearing his glasses. But all of their classmates only shook their heads or said no.

When class ended for the day, Ms. Moriarty asked Zach and Zoe if they'd had any luck solving the mystery of their deflated football. They told her they thought the glasses would be a clue, but no one in their class was missing a pair.

"But somebody in the school might be," Ms. Moriarty said. "I'll ask around. Think of me as an assistant detective."

"We can use all the help we can get!" Zach said.

Zoe nodded. "We *have* to figure this out before Thanksgiving break."

"Even if we only have one more day," Zach reminded her.

Zoe turned to her brother and gave him a high five, just without the jump this time. They hadn't won anything yet.

"Plenty of time," she said with a wave of her hand.

"She's not only determined," her brother said to Ms. Moriarty. "She's pretty confident."

Ms. Moriarty smiled.

"I've sort of picked up on that by now," she said. "With both of you."

FIVE

The next day was Wednesday, the day before Thanksgiving.

As soon as Zach and Zoe got to school, they put up a note about the missing glasses on the bulletin board in the lobby. It said anyone who lost a pair should see Ms. Moriarty to retrieve them. Zach and Zoe weren't giving up on the glasses being a clue just yet. Partly because they never gave up, but also because they knew it could still lead to something.

Even though the school was letting them out early that afternoon for the holiday, there was still time for recess. Mateo brought his own ball to school again. As soon as the bell rang, they were on their way outside to have a football game.

It was a really good game. This time Jimmy decided not to play, and went over to the jungle gym instead. But Zach and Zoe were more excited than ever, because the Turkey Bowl was tomorrow, and this was their last practice. Their classmates even let them play on the same team.

On the last play of the game, Zoe played quarterback. She was excited to have the practice in case she got to play quarterback in the Turkey Bowl.

"You've always got to have your arm ready," Zach said to his sister.

"Oh, it's ready all right," she said, just before she threw him the long pass that won the game for their team.

When they got back inside, they realized the game had ended early today. So Zoe asked Ms. Moriarty if she could take one more look around the storage room. She was still convinced that the answers she was looking for were in there somewhere.

And she had been promising Zach, and promising herself, that she was going to solve the mystery before the end of the school day. Now, with recess over, she was running out of time.

Ms. Moriarty opened the door to the storage room, and Zoe spotted the deflated ball where she had left it at the top of the pile. She picked it up and studied the place near the laces where Zach had discovered the hole. Zoe put her hand on the laces, smiling, remembering the feeling that she'd gotten when she threw the winning touchdown pass just moments ago.

Her dad was right. Part of the magic of sports was the memories. Sometimes just holding a football in your hand could make a good memory come flooding back. It was as if the play or the game you were remembering happened all over again.

Now Zoe stared at the ball, hard, and spoke to it in the empty room.

"Come *on*," she said softly. "How about a little help here?"

She was about to toss it back into the bin when she noticed something she hadn't before:

A small streak of green ink, just visible underneath the laces, and near the small hole in the ball.

She wasn't sure what it meant. But she was convinced it had to mean something. Maybe somebody put the hole in the ball with a green pen.

Normally she didn't think it was possible for the tip of a ballpoint pen to put a hole in a football. But when she felt how soft the rubber of their old football was, she believed it was more than possible with this ball. That was why she was sure the green ink was her best clue yet, even better than the pair of glasses she found with Zach.

She ran out of the storage room as fast as she would run down the field trying to win the Turkey Bowl.

SIX

As soon as Zoe found Zach in the hallway, she told him about the green ink on the football.

Zach grinned.

"You found a clue without me," he said, more impressed than disappointed. "And that's making me green with envy!"

"Be serious," she said.

Zach grinned. "Can't I be funny and serious at the same time?"

"What's *not* going to be funny," Zoe said, "is trying to see who uses green ink before it's time to go home."

"But someone in another class could be using green ink, too," Zach said.

"I thought of that," Zoe said. "But to get to the end of the mystery, we have to start somewhere."

She turned to walk back into their classroom, but Zach stopped her.

"What are we going to do if someone *is* using green ink?" he asked, concerned.

"I don't know," Zoe said. "Sometimes, as much as I want to find out what happened, I'm afraid to find out what happened. Especially if one of our friends put the hole in the ball."

"Well," Zach said, "you know what Mom says. If you keep putting one foot in front of another, you'll never get ahead of yourself."

"Exactly," Zoe agreed.

All the kids in class were seated at their desks. Zach and Zoe were in the front row. Mateo and Malik and Lily and Kari were behind them. Jimmy was in the back row next to Brian Koppelman.

Zoe thought it was almost as if Jimmy got picked last when the desks were assigned.

Their last assignment before Thanksgiving was to write down the things they were most grateful for this year. Ms. Moriarty handed out note cards and said she wanted everyone to write about what they had in their lives that mattered to them most.

"Thinking about these things and writing them down will get us all into the spirit of giving thanks," she said.

Zoe quickly scribbled down her list. She knew exactly what she was thankful for: her family, her friends, her health, her teachers, and her love of a good mystery.

Ms. Moriarty gave the class permission to talk among themselves while writing. She even encouraged them to share their ideas if one of them was struggling. Zach's list was the same as Zoe's, except he had left out the part about mysteries and put down "sports" instead.

"Let's see if we can solve the mystery right now," Zoe whispered.

"One written in green ink," Zach whispered back.

Ms. Moriarty announced it was almost time to collect the note cards. She wasn't going to grade them, she said. She wanted all the kids in class to show their parents what they'd written. But she wanted to read them before they left school today. It gave Zoe a great idea: She asked Ms. Moriarty if she could collect all the cards. That way she could see what color pens all of her classmates had used.

"That would be very helpful, Zoe. Thank you," said Ms. Moriarty.

Zoe got up from her seat and began making her way through the rows of desks.

She noticed Malik and Mateo had both used pens with blue ink. Lily, who loved being colorful, had used purple. Kari used orange.

There was only one person in the whole class using a green pen:

Jimmy Evans, in the back row.

But Zoe knew not to get ahead of herself. Just because a pen is green on the outside doesn't mean it writes in green ink.

Zoe picked up his card, not looking to see what he'd written, only peeking to check if it was written in green ink. Sure enough, it was. It didn't mean Jimmy had the only green pen in the whole school. But he did have the only one in their class.

As Zoe came back up the aisle, she made eye contact with her brother and nodded.

They both knew that just because Jimmy was the only one writing with green ink didn't mean he had put the hole in the ball. Zoe made sure to continue putting one foot in front of another and not get ahead of herself.

But sometimes the only way to find the right answer was to ask the right question.

SEVEN

Zoe brought the stack of cards up to Ms. Moriarty, who began reading them to herself. She told the class they could talk quietly while she read.

"What are we going to do?" Zach whispered to his sister.

Zoe looked over at Jimmy. "We have to at least ask if he knows anything," she said.

"But what if we're wrong?"

Zoe shrugged. "Then we'll know to cross Jimmy off our list of suspects and keep looking for clues. We still don't know who the glasses belong to."

"It's a mystery," Zach said, and winked at Zoe.

A few minutes later, the bell sounded. All the kids got up to gather their stuff. Ms. Moriarty stood by the door, handing cards back to each student as they left. Jimmy was one of the last kids in the classroom, putting things away in his cubby. He threw on his jacket and grabbed his backpack. By the time he finished, the only people left in the classroom were Zach, Zoe, Jimmy, and Ms. Moriarty.

Zach and Zoe walked over to Jimmy.

"Hi, Jimmy," Zoe said.

"Hi," he said back.

"You know," Zach said, "we're still trying to solve the mystery of how the hole ended up in that old football."

Zoe thought Jimmy looked nervous all of a sudden, but wasn't sure. The way she still wasn't sure he'd put the hole in the ball. Maybe Jimmy was just a nervous kid.

"Any luck?" Jimmy asked.

"Well, as a matter of fact, I thought I did have a piece of luck today," she said. "There was a pen mark on the ball that I hadn't noticed before."

She made sure not to say that it had been green ink. She didn't want to accuse him of something he hadn't done. That would be much worse than putting a small hole in a football.

"But does just finding ink help you find out how the hole got in the ball?" Jimmy asked.

"Not necessarily," Zoe said. "But it might."

"You know what?" Zach said. "The person who did it might not even know they did it."

Suddenly, though, Jimmy was looking everywhere in the room except at Zach and Zoe. He looked even more nervous than he did that day when Zoe had thrown him the ball.

Now he looked as if he was trying as hard as he could not to look at Zoe, or Zach.

"It's green ink, isn't it?" Jimmy said finally.

Zoe told him that it was.

"I never meant to put a hole in the ball," Jimmy said in a quiet voice, head down.

"And we don't even care that you did," Zoe said. "An old football will never be more important to us than a friend."

"I'm your friend?" he said, looking up now.

"Of course you are," said Zoe.

And the best time to be a friend, Zach and Zoe's parents had always taught them, was when somebody needed one most. They could tell Jimmy Evans needed a couple right now.

Zach and Zoe could see Ms. Moriarty watching them from her desk. They knew she could probably hear what was happening in the back of the room. But the Walker twins also knew that although Ms. Moriarty was their teacher, she believed the best way for them to learn was to find the right answers on their own.

Jimmy said, "I just finally got mad at always being picked last. It's why I went to the jungle gym today. I didn't want to get picked last again."

Zoe was the one who spoke first, beating Zach to it.

"And you know what?" she said. "My brother and I should have done something about you being picked last all the time."

She wanted to take the pressure off Jimmy and put it on Zach and herself. Zach obviously wanted to do the same thing.

"We should have been more sensitive about that," Zach said.

"You don't have to say that," Jimmy said, looking down.

"Forget about saying something," Zoe said. "We should have *done* something."

There was still time before they had to get on their buses. Jimmy sat back down at his desk. Zach and Zoe sat down at desks on either side of him.

"Nobody ever seems to want me on their team," Jimmy said. "No one ever wants to throw me the ball, because they're afraid I'll drop it."

"I threw you the ball," Zoe said.

Jimmy managed a small smile. "And I dropped it!" he said. "I really like playing football. I'm just not very good at it."

"You can get better," Zoe said. "You just have to practice more."

"You guys have each other to practice with," Jimmy said. "I don't have anybody right now."

"What about your parents?" Zach asked.

"Oh, my dad would throw a ball around with me if he were here," Jimmy said. "But he's in the army, fighting all the way over on the other side of the world. And with him gone, my mom never has any time."

Jimmy Evans had never mentioned that his dad was in the army until now. There were lots of things about him Zach and Zoe didn't know, and wished they'd found out.

"Sounds to me like your dad is a hero," Zoe said.

"He is!" Jimmy said. "But it doesn't make me miss him any less. Thinking about him just makes me sad. But the other day it made me mad, too."

"And you took it out on the ball?" Zach guessed.

Jimmy nodded.

"I had stayed after school on Friday because there was a meeting in the cafeteria for kids who might want to join the Cub Scouts," he said. "I told my mom that being a scout was something I was sure Dad would want me to do. I'd even get to wear a uniform."

"So what happened at the meeting?" Zoe asked, curious.

"I thought it was just going to be kids," Jimmy said. "But there were a lot of dads there, too. Some of them are scout leaders. It just made me miss my own dad even more."

"I'm so sorry," Zach said.

"Not as sorry as I am for what happened next," Jimmy said.

While he was waiting for his mom to pick him up, he happened to pass by the storage room. The door was partially open. Their football was sitting on top of the pile in the bin. He was feeling bad already about being picked last again that day, and missing the ball Zoe had thrown to him.

Before he even realized what he was doing, he was jabbing the green ballpoint pen he'd pulled out of his pocket into the ball. He didn't even know he'd actually put a hole in it until Zach found the deflated ball.

"I am so sorry," he said. "I wish I'd said something, but I was too ashamed."

"Forget it," Zach said.

"And we're sorry that you've been feeling this way," Zoe said.

"As a matter of fact," Zach said, realizing he'd come up with a brilliant idea in that moment, "that is why we're going to ask if you can come play in our family's touch football game tomorrow at our house."

Now Jimmy really smiled.

"Do you mean it?" he said, eyes wide.

"We try to never say anything we don't mean," Zoe said, looking at her brother.

"You're sure you're not doing it because you think you have to?" Jimmy asked.

"We're doing it," Zach said, "because we want to."

"And because you're our friend," Zoe added.

She looked past Jimmy to the front of their classroom. The biggest smile in the room belonged to Ms. Moriarty.

EIGHT

The Walkers' annual Turkey Bowl football game was scheduled to start at noon in their backyard. That gave Tess and Danny Walker plenty of time to finish cooking before the game, and everyone a chance to wash up before dinner.

"It's a good thing we play before we eat and not after," Grandpa Richie said as they warmed up. "If we didn't, all that turkey and fixings and pie might slow me down."

"No, we wouldn't want that," Danny Walker said, grinning at his dad. "You ought to get the chance to show off all that speed you passed on to the rest of us."

"It's more than speed," Grandpa Richie said. "You've got to have the moves, too, like I did in basketball."

"Sometimes making those moves just seems to take you a little longer in football," Zoe teased.

"Hey!" her grandfather said. "Whose side are you on?"

Jimmy and his mom had arrived at their house a few minutes earlier. The night before, Zach and Zoe came home and told their mom about inviting Jimmy to the Turkey Bowl. Tess Walker then called Mrs. Evans to ask about her Thanksgiving dinner plans. Mrs. Evans said she had planned to cook up a small turkey, but the truth was that the holidays just weren't the same with Jimmy's father overseas. Tess had an idea: Mrs. Evans should drop their turkey off at one of the churches in Middletown where the homeless were served Thanksgiving dinners. Then they were invited to have Thanksgiving dinner with the Walker family after the game.

"It must be so hard, not knowing when your husband is coming home," Tess said to Jimmy's mom.

"We don't care when it is," Mrs. Evans said, "as long as he's safe."

Because their own families were having late dinners today, Malik, Mateo, and Mateo's dad also dropped by to join the game. They had enough players for five on each team. Usually Grandpa Richie and Danny Walker picked the teams. But today, in honor of Jimmy and his mom joining the game, Grandpa Richie announced that they would be team captains.

Mrs. Evans said that Jimmy could choose first.

"Can I make two picks?" he asked.

"Sure," Danny Walker said. "In the Turkey Bowl, we pretty much make up the rules as we go."

"Then I pick Zach *and* Zoe," he said.

"Well," Grandpa Richie said, "that team is loaded with talent already."

Mrs. Evans took Malik and Mateo with her first two picks. Jimmy then picked Grandpa Richie and Mateo's dad. Jimmy's mom rounded out the teams by picking Zach and Zoe's mom, and finally their dad.

Zoe whispered to Jimmy, "My dad got picked last today, and he's the best player in the game."

Jimmy just smiled in response.

Danny Walker had bought a special new ball for this year's game, with "Turkey Bowl" printed on the side. It was decided beforehand that the first team to score five touchdowns won. Before they started, Danny Walker looked at the twins. "Please tell everybody the only rules for the game that matter."

"Play hard," Zach said.

"Have fun," said Zoe.

"And nobody get hurt," Danny Walker said.

"Especially me!" Grandpa Richie yelled.

Even though it was the end of November, it felt almost like a summer day. The sun was high in the sky over the yard and there was a slight breeze. It just seemed like perfect football weather. This was the Walker family's favorite football day of the whole year. They were all together with family and friends, and they hadn't even sat down to dinner yet.

Zach and Zoe's team got the ball first. Grandpa Richie was the quarterback. Zach and Zoe had told him the night before about Jimmy, and how nobody ever wanted to throw him the ball at recess. With that in mind, Grandpa Richie didn't waste any time.

"Let's see what the new guy's got," he said.

He positioned Zach and Zoe on one side of the field. Jimmy was on the other. Grandpa Richie told Jimmy to run down about five yards and cut to the inside.

He dropped back. Jimmy made his cut. Grandpa Richie threw him the ball. Not only did Jimmy catch it, he ran for ten more yards before Mateo caught up with him and stopped him from going all the way for a touchdown.

When Jimmy got back to the huddle, he looked as if he'd caught a pass

in the Super Bowl. The smile on his face was like Christmas had come early. Everybody on their team high-fived him.

Zach scored on the next play. When Jimmy's mom's team got the ball, Danny Walker faked a pass to Malik and then threw a long pass to Zach and Zoe's mom, who looked even happier than Jimmy had when she scored a touchdown.

There were so many good plays from both teams. But there was even more laughter. They were all doing what Danny Walker had told them to do: playing hard and having fun. Not only was no one getting hurt, but no one's feelings were getting hurt, either.

The game was tied 3–3 when Grandpa Richie called for a trick play. Zach would start out as quarterback. When Zoe snapped him the ball, Zach would run to his left, stop, and then throw the ball back across the field to Grandpa Richie, who'd be ready in the backfield. You could only throw one forward pass in football on the same play. That meant Zach had to make sure his grandfather was behind him before throwing him the ball.

The plan then was for Grandpa Richie to throw a long pass to Jimmy.

"Run as far as you can as fast as you can and I'll get it to you," Grandpa Richie said to Jimmy.

"I'll try my best," Jimmy said.

Grandpa Richie put a hand on his shoulder, smiled, and said, "Haven't seen anybody in this game trying harder than you today."

The play worked just the way Grandpa Richie thought it would. Zach threw a perfect spiral to Grandpa Richie, who was standing a few yards behind him. Everybody on defense came running for Zach and Zoe's grandfather, thinking he was the only receiver on the play. But then, he stopped and threw it to Jimmy near the end zone, who had no one from the other team even close to him.

After the game, Zach and Zoe would admit they were afraid Jimmy was *too* open and had *too* much time to think about catching the ball without dropping it. But Jimmy gathered it in as if he had the surest hands in all of Middletown, and ran for a touchdown. It was at that moment they all heard clapping from the gate to the Walkers' backyard.

They turned and saw that it was a tall man in an army uniform.

No one said anything until Jimmy Evans yelled, "Dad!" and started running across the backyard, the ball still tucked under his arm. He held on to it as he jumped into his father's arms.

NINE

Jimmy was laughing and crying at the same time. Mrs. Evans had her arms around Jimmy and his dad, squeezing tightly.

Nobody else in the Walkers' backyard could believe what they were seeing.

"How?" Mrs. Evans finally managed to say, tears beginning to drip down her face.

"I found out two days ago," Sergeant Evans said. "There were so many airplane connections I wasn't sure if I could make it back in time. So I didn't want to get any-body's hopes up. But I figured that if I did make it back by Thanksgiving, it would be a pretty great surprise."

Jimmy held his father tight. Sergeant Evans had one arm around his son and the other wrapped around his wife.

"When I got home, the lights were off and no one was there. So I asked the neighbor where to find you guys. Glad I didn't miss the biggest football game of the year," he said, winking at Jimmy.

"So are we," Danny Walker said. "Thank you for being here today. And thank you for your service, sir." He shook Sergeant Evans's hand.

Zoe turned to her brother then and said, "Are you thinking what I'm thinking?"

"I usually am," Zach said, grinning.

At the exact same time they shouted, *"Best Thanksgiving ever!"*

Suddenly, Grandpa Richie looked at Jimmy's dad and said, "Can I ask you for one favor, sir?"

Jimmy's dad grinned. "Sure," he said.

"How about you take my place as quarterback. I think I wore out my arm throwing that long pass to your son."

"It would be my pleasure," Sergeant Evans said. "I haven't had a chance to play much football lately."

"This might be the greatest substitution in Turkey Bowl history," Danny Walker said.

"Maybe in football history," said Tess.

"One thing is for sure," Danny Walker said. "No one ever traveled farther to get into a game."

Jimmy's mom's team had the ball. Danny Walker threw her another long pass, which she caught down the field for a quick touchdown, tying the game 4–4.

The game came down to the final play. The ball now belonged to Zach and Zoe's team.

In the huddle Sergeant Evans said, "All of you try to get open. My arm's a little rusty, but I'll try to throw it to one of you."

"Not one of us," Zoe said. "Jimmy."

"No doubt," Zach said.

"How are you guys so sure?" Jimmy asked.

"My brother and I are pretty big on how stories are supposed to end," Zoe said. "And we're both pretty sure how this one is supposed to end today."

Zach and Zoe said they'd line up on the right, and told Jimmy to line up on the left. Then they'd crisscross in the middle of the field during the play.

Zoe hiked the ball to Sergeant Evans and ran across the field with Zach, while Jimmy ran the other way. Zach and Zoe were both open.

They just weren't nearly as open as Jimmy was.

He ran free toward the back of the yard. It turned out his dad's arm wasn't rusty at all. He threw the best spiral anybody had thrown all day. Jimmy reached up for the ball and brought it in to his chest. He crossed the goal line with the touchdown that won the Turkey Bowl for his team.

He came running for his dad one more time and jumped into his arms, holding on like he'd never let go. Meanwhile, Grandpa Richie and Danny Walker huddled up and announced that Jimmy Evans was the most valuable player in this year's Turkey Bowl.

Not only was he the MVP, but Zach and Zoe's dad agreed that Jimmy should keep the ball.

Afterward, Malik, Mateo, and his dad said their good-byes before heading home to have dinner with their own families. Everyone else went inside to wash up, and watched pro football on television until dinner was ready.

After Tess Walker said grace, Sergeant Evans said he had an announcement he wanted to make.

He cleared his throat. "When I come home next, for Christmas," he said, "I'm coming home for good."

"I knew it!" Jimmy shouted from beside his father. "I knew if I just wished hard enough for my dream, it would come true."

He reached into his pocket then and brought out a note card. It was his Thanksgiving writing assignment from school.

He read it aloud to everybody sitting around the table.

"'I'm thankful for my mom and my dad. But I'd be *really* thankful if my dad came home.'"

Zach and Zoe looked at each other, the same thought inside their heads:

Green ink had never looked so good.

TEN

It was time for recess on the first Monday after Thanksgiving break. The weather wasn't as warm as it had been on Thanksgiving Day, but everybody was still anxious to get outside and run around.

They didn't have a new football to play with yet, so they were hoping Mateo had brought his from home again.

As they left the cafeteria with the rest of their classmates, Zoe pulled Zach aside. She looked disappointed.

"Why don't you look happy?" asked Zach. "We just had an awesome Thanksgiving and Turkey Bowl! Plus four days off school!"

"I'm glad we solved the football fiasco," she said. "But we still don't know who the glasses we found belong to."

"That's true," said Zach. "But we did put up that flyer, and no one's come to claim them."

"I know," she said. "I just wish there was some way to solve that mystery, too."

Zach patted his sister on the back. "Maybe we will. But for now, let's just go out there and have fun."

Zoe agreed.

All of a sudden, Mr. Parker came jogging down the hallway from the other direction, something hidden behind his back. He proudly showed them what he was carrying in his hand:

A can of something called "Fix a Flat," which he described as "magic goop" that was supposed to seal up holes in flat tires. But he figured it could work on footballs too.

"Thanks, Mr. Parker," Jimmy said from behind him. "But we're not going to need our old football today."

Mr. Parker looked confused. So did the other kids.

Jimmy told everybody to wait where they were while he ran back to his cubby. When he came back, out of breath, he showed them all the Turkey Bowl ball he'd won for being MVP.

"I'm giving this one to our class as an early Christmas present," Jimmy said. "This will be our game ball at school from now on."

"Wait," Zach said. "You earned that ball."

"We gave it to you because of the way our team won the game," Zoe said.

"And now I'm giving it back," he said. "My parents say it's better to give than receive. And you both know I already received the greatest gift I'm ever going to get because of my dad."

"Well, if it's okay with you . . ." Zoe said.

". . . I guess it's okay with us," Zach finished.

Jimmy smiled at them.

"Besides," he said, "I owed you one."

All the kids gathered around Jimmy to thank him and admire their new ball. Zach and Zoe stood apart, toward the entrance to the cafeteria, smiling. That's when Zoe noticed something out of the corner of her eye.

She turned to peek inside the cafeteria and saw Ms. Gundy, arms crossed, pacing the floor. Perched on her nose sat the glasses Zach and Zoe found in the ball bin.

Zoe gently shoved her brother to catch his attention. He turned, and when he noticed Ms. Gundy, his eyes lit up.

Suddenly, Ms. Moriarty appeared behind them. "Ms. Gundy came into my classroom right after you left on Wednesday." The twins turned to face her. "I didn't have time to tell you. She dropped her glasses when she was cleaning the recess equipment last Friday after lunch. Including your football."

Zach and Zoe looked at each other, stunned. "That was pretty nice of her," said Zach.

"Sometimes, people aren't all that they seem on the outside," Ms. Moriarty said, smiling.

Zach and Zoe were happy Ms. Gundy found her glasses, and vowed never to call her Ms. Grumpy again, even in secret.

Ms. Moriarty turned to leave, and Zach and Zoe filed out the door with their classmates. Finally, it was time to play some football.

They walked outside together. It was Zoe's turn to be one of the captains today, and it was time to choose sides.

Zoe looked around at all the players and thought for a moment. She made her decision, and it was a no-brainer. "Jimmy Evans," she called.

JOIN THE TEAM.
SOLVE THE CASE!

Help Zach and Zoe
get to the bottom of another mystery!

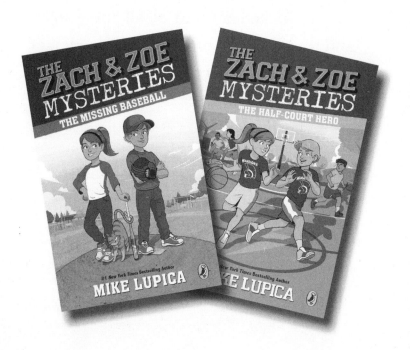